Olly Spellmaker and the Hairy Horror

Susan Price started writing and telling stories when she was very young – and was winning prizes for it from the age of fourteen. Her first novel, *The Devil's Piper*, was bought by a publisher when she was sixteen. Since then, she has had lots of jobs and written many books for children and young adults, including *The Sterkarm Handshake* (which won the Guardian Children's Fiction Award) and *The Ghost Drum* (which won the Carnegie Medal).

Visit Susan Price's website at www.susanprice.org.uk

Shock Shop is a superb collection of short, illustrated, scary books for younger readers by some of today's most acclaimed writers for children.

Also by Susan Price from Macmillan

Olly Spellmaker and the Sulky Smudge

SHOCK SHOP

Olly Spellmaker and the Hairy Horror

Susan Price

Illustrated by David Roberts

MACMILLAN CHILDREN'S BOOKS

First published as *Hairy Bill* in 2002 by Macmillan Children's Books

This edition published 2004 by Macmillan Children's Books
a division of Macmillan Publishers Limited
20 New Wharf Road, London N1 9RR
Basingstoke and Oxford
www.panmacmillan.com

Associated companies throughout the world

ISBN 0 330 42119 0

3 5 7 9 8 6 4 2

A CIP catalogue record for this book is available from
the British Library.

Printed and bound in Great Britain by Mackays of Chatham plc, Kent

Contents

Chapter 1
Something Comes Down the Chimney   1

Chapter 2
The Break-in   9

Chapter 3
Things That Dust in the Night   23

Chapter 4
Miss Spellmaker   34

Chapter 5
The Bargain   57

Chapter 6
The Dragon and the Mouse   66

Chapter 7
Blessings Be   80

Chapter 1
Something Comes Down the Chimney

It was a cold night. The room was dark except for the light coming from the landing, through an open crack of door. Alex, curled up in bed, was just getting warm enough to drop off to sleep. Outside, a car door slammed and an alarm chirupped as it was set. Much closer, something slithered inside the chimney.

Alex's eyes opened and stayed alert. He stiffened into stillness, and waited, and listened.

Inside the chimney, a voice muttered, annoyed. Something scratched and slipped on

1

the brickwork. Old dust and soot spattered into the grate.

Alex snatched a breath to shout, but then held it. If he made a noise, whatever was coming down the chimney would know he was there, and exactly where to find him. If he kept quiet, maybe it would think the room was empty and go away.

He had never liked having a fireplace in his bedroom. What was the point, when he never had a fire? But his mother said it was 'a lovely old feature of the house'. His father always said that it was 'handy for Father Christmas', but whatever was muttering and scratching in the chimney, it wasn't Father Christmas.

He heard a thump in the grate. Whatever it was had landed in the hearth. There was a cough, and an angry tutting. Then another thump, this time on the floor. It was out of the chimney and in the room.

Footsteps coming across the room! Alex snatched a frightened breath and almost choked. The blankets twitched against his leg. The duvet was moving, was being pulled down! Alex squeaked and grabbed at it, terrified that he might be uncovered. But with one strong tug, the cover was yanked from his fingers.

By his bed stood a dark shape, no taller than him, but wide. And hairy. Lots of long, shaggy hair hung down past its thick shoulders. The light from behind it made the hair into a halo. One big hand held up the duvet. The face was hidden in the shadows, and what it was like, Alex couldn't tell.

He could feel his heart jumping about under his collarbone. What was it? What was it going to do? Eat him?

It spoke. Whatever it was that had come

down the chimney spoke to him; but the voice was so grumbling and deep that he couldn't understand it. Alex just squeaked again.

Whatever-It-Was spoke a second time, and this time he understood. "Is your name Matheson?" it said.

Alex was so surprised that, for a moment, he stopped being scared. He had never imagined that monsters would ask your name before they ate you. Maybe they had to make sure they didn't eat the wrong person? "No!"

"Och!" said the thing, very annoyed. Alex realized that it had a Scottish accent, like his mother.

"My mother's named Matheson," he said, though he didn't know why. He had a confused idea that he'd better tell the truth because, being a monster, and magical and supernatural, it would know if he lied. And if the thing was looking for a Matheson, maybe it would leave him alone and go off to find

4

his mother – though that was a cowardly thought, and he was ashamed.

"Is her name Kirsty Matheson?"

"Yes!" Alex said.

"Is she of the Black Isle Mathesons?"

"Er . . ."Alex didn't know what it was talking about until he suddenly remembered his mother showing him some old photographs and telling him that her grandfather – or had it been her great-grandfather? – had been a farmer in Scotland, in a place called 'The Black Isle'. "Yes!" he said.

The thing's eyes seemed to open wide – at least, they caught the light for a second. "At fine last! Home!" It came forward, and Alex cowered back, but the thing only tossed the duvet into the air and spread it over him. Alex was glad to hide under the cover, but the thing pulled it off his head. "Tell your mother that her Auntie Jeanie went home last night, and so I've come to serve her."

"All right," Alex gasped, ready to agree to

anything, if it left him alone.

The thing picked up a cup from the bedside table, a cup stained with the hot chocolate Alex had brought up to bed with him. "Tch!" said the thing, annoyed. "Tch!" Taking the cup, it tramped across the bedroom and out of the door, vanishing into the light of the landing.

Alex covered his head and lay still, waiting to see if it would come back. A long time – it seemed an agonizingly long time – went by, and he thought of shouting for his dad, but didn't, because the thing might come back before his dad could climb the stairs. But then he heard his dad's footsteps. He waited until they reached the landing, then sat up and shouted.

His dad pushed open the bedroom door, letting in a flood of bright light. "What's up?"

"Something came down the chimney, Dad! It took my cup!"

His dad sat on the end of his bed. "Something came down the chimney and took your cup? Now, why would anything want your cup?"

Alex told him how he had heard the noises in the chimney; how the blankets had been pulled from him by a shaggy thing that had asked him his name . . . It made him angry when his dad started to laugh. "It's true!"

"You were having a bad dream."

"But it took my cup." Alex pointed to the bedside table, where the cup had been. There was nothing there now except his alarm clock.

"Your mum must have taken it. She came up not long ago and looked in on you."

"When? I didn't hear her."

"Because you were asleep," his dad said.

"Oh," said Alex. Perhaps he had been dreaming, then. He felt silly.

His father leaned over and kissed the top of his head. "Back to sleep, eh? I'll lie down by you, shall I, and stay until you're asleep?"

"All right, then." Alex lay down. He did feel sleepy. His father stretched himself out at the side of him, and it was nice having him there. Alex was asleep when his father crept back downstairs.

It was the next morning when they realized it hadn't been a dream.

Chapter 2
The Break-in

It was Saturday the next morning, but Alex was woken from his lie-in by his mother yelling for his father. "Rob! Rob!" She sounded scared.

The bathroom door opened and Rob Langford shouted, "What's up now?"

Kirsty Matheson yelled back, "We've been broken into!"

Rob exclaimed, and rushed downstairs with a pounding of feet. Alex jumped out of bed himself, his heart beating a little faster than usual, and followed his dad.

The narrow hallway seemed full of his father, who was striding up and down between the front door and the kitchen, waving his arms. "Where did they get in?"

"I don't know!" Kirsty was in the kitchen. "But somebody's been in."

Rob stood still. "Why? What makes you think so?"

"Well," said Kirsty. "Everything's so . . ." – she waved her arms – " . . . so tidy."

Alex looked into the living room. It *was* tidier than usual. There were no old newspapers or magazines lying anywhere, and all the videos and CDs had been put away. The carpet looked freshly swept, and cushions were placed neatly on the sofa and chairs. In the far corner, by the bay window, the computer had been covered, and the chair pushed under the computer desk.

From the kitchen his mother said, "The washing-up's been done. And the washing. Everything's been put away." Just as Alex crowded into the small kitchen behind his father, she said, "The pantry's been tidied."

"It's the first time," said Rob, "that I ever

10

heard of burglars who broke in and *tidied up*."

Alex squirmed between his parents and got through to the sink. In the drainer were stacked plates and cutlery and bowls. And there was his mug, with the dinosaurs on it. He picked it up. "Look."

"What?" said his mother.

"It's my mug."

"I can see it's your mug, Alex! We're busy!"

"I mean," Alex said, "that it wasn't down here last night. I took it upstairs with me, didn't I? I had hot chocolate in it."

His parents stared at him, his mother more mystified than his father.

"Remember me telling you about the thing that came down the chimney?"

"Alex, that was a dream! Your mother fetched the mug—"

"I didn't fetch the mug," Kirsty said.

They all looked at each other.

"When you went upstairs," Rob said, "you

didn't bring his mug down and wash it?"

"I looked in at his door, but I didn't go inside," she replied. "I didn't bring his mug down. I didn't wash it."

Alex waved the clean mug in the air. "But here it is! I told you, Dad. The hairy thing that came down the chimney took it."

"And brought it downstairs and washed it up?" his father said.

"Well, I didn't do any of this washing-up," Kirsty said. "Did you? I didn't put these clothes in the washer. I didn't tidy these shelves. I didn't—"

"Alex," his father said, "tell us about your dream again."

"It wasn't a dream."

"Tell us about it anyway."

So, as they stood in the kitchen, Alex told again how he'd heard the noises in the chimney, and how the duvet had been pulled off him, and he'd seen this short, hairy figure standing by his bed. "Then it asked me if my name was Matheson, and when I said no, that it was *your* name, it asked if you were one of the Black Isle Mathesons—"

"Oh!" Kirsty Matheson said. They looked at her. She'd put her hands to her face.

"When I said yes," Alex went on, "it said, 'Home!' And it picked up my mug and went, 'Tch!' like it shouldn't be there. And it went out of the room. Oh – and it said to tell you that your Auntie Jeanie had gone home."

"Oh!" said Kirsty Matheson. "Hairy Bill!"

They looked at her again. "What?" Rob asked.

"Hairy Bill," she said. "Oh – make me a cup of coffee and I'll tell you."

So Alex filled the kettle at the tap, while his father spooned coffee into cups, and a few minutes later they carried the coffee into the living room. Alex brought some bananas, too, as breakfast.

Kirsty was sitting on the settee, and they sat either side of her.

13

"You know my great-grandfather was a farmer in the Black Isle," she said. "They'd farmed there – oh, for ever. There've always been Mathesons in the Black Isle. Well, the farm was haunted. By a bogle. Called Hairy Bill."

"Haunted by a bogle?" Alex said. He thought that places could only be haunted by ghosts.

"A bogle is a sort of ghost," his father said.

"I was told lots of stories about Hairy Bill," Kirsty said. "I believed it when I was little, but after I grew up, I thought it was just a story."

14

"You never told me about any bogle," Alex said.

"I have told you, Alex, but you never seemed much interested."

"As the story goes, Hairy Bill used to do a lot of work round the farm," Rob said. "Your great-grandmother – no, she would be your great-great-grandmother, Al – had to leave food for him. Bread and milk. Then he'd sweep up the hearth and lay the fire ready for morning, and do the washing-up." He looked at Kirsty. "That right?"

She nodded. "He'd help with the harvest, groom the horses, milk the cows – he'd do any sort of work. But on special occasions, like birthdays and weddings and Christmas, he had to have cake and cream. Heaven help them if they forgot him!"

"Why?" Alex asked nervously.

"Instead of tidying up, he'd turn the place upside-down," Kirsty said. "Instead of helping the butter come, he'd sour the milk. He'd

15

tie the horses' tails in knots, and stop the cows milking and the hens laying."

"We're all right, then," Alex said, lying on his back and kicking his legs in the air. "We haven't got any hens or cows and we don't make butter."

His parents didn't seem amused. They both looked glum.

"Poor Auntie Jeanie," Kirsty said. "She was the last of them – the last of Great-grandad's children."

"Why's she gone home?" Alex asked.

"It means she's died, Alex. And now she's dead, Hairy Bill's moved on to us. He always moves on to somebody else in the family."

"Great!" Alex said. He looked round at the tidy room. "We've got a ghost that clears up!"

"Not great," said his mother, shaking her head. "Not great at all."

"But think! If you just leave him some bread and milk, you'll never have to do any washing-up again! And he'll wash the windows and run the cleaner round and dust—"

"But it's easy to offend bogles," said Kirsty. "They're touchy. And they get bored with being helpful. I don't want to be haunted."

"Hard luck," Alex said. "We're stuck with him."

"Oh no, we're not," his mother said. "We can lay him."

"We can what?"

"Lay him. That's what it's called when you get rid of a ghost – 'laying the ghost'."

"You can't get rid of our very own family ghost!" Alex said.

"I'm going to, though," his mother said, and she got up and went over to the computer. Pulling out the chair, she sat down and took the cloth from over the monitor. "You two can make breakfast. I just want to check something."

They made porridge with raisins. Alex and his dad ate in the kitchen, but Kirsty insisted on eating as she sat in front of the computer. She'd entered 'bogle' into a search engine, and had come up with a lot of folklore and legend sites.

"I don't want to get rid of Hairy Bill," Alex said to his father.

"You didn't like it when he came down the chimney."

"I didn't know who he was, then."

"I don't want to live with a ghost any more than your mum does," Rob said. "They're all right in films and books, but a bit of a bore in real life."

"It's not fair," Alex said. "Nobody cares what I think."

They left their bowls on the counter and went through into the other room. Leaning on the back of Kirsty's chair, Rob asked, "What have you gleaned?"

The computer screen was filled with Celtic scrollwork on a green, marbled background. In between the scrolls were bits of text.

"Listen to this," Kirsty said, and she read aloud from the screen. As she read, she moved the cursor with the mouse, so they could follow the words.

"'The brownie or bogle must be given his daily wage of bread and milk in return for his services, but any further offering or any hint of reward invariably drives the creature away.

'Some say this is because God made bogles to be the servants of mankind, and it is their fate to serve without payment, while others say that no gift of human manufacture can be good enough for one of the fairy tribe, to which the bogle belongs. Whatever the reason, the infallible way to lay a bogle is to leave them a gift, especially one of clothes.' So

19

that's what we'll do. We'll leave out some clothes. Have you got some old stuff you don't want, Rob?"

"Dad's clothes'll be too big," Alex said. "Hairy's only about as big as me."

"You've got some old clothes," his mother said. "I'll put them out tonight, and that'll be that. Hairy Bill can go and find some other Matheson to bother." She held out her porridge bowl. "Take that into the kitchen for me, will you, please?"

When Alex went into the kitchen, he found that the porridge bowls he and his father had left on the counter had been washed and placed in the drainer. He put his mother's bowl in the sink, and said, "Here's another one for you to wash." Then he had to turn suddenly and look behind him. He couldn't help it, he was so sure someone was behind him.

No one else was in the kitchen. But Hairy Bill was somewhere close by, invisible. He had to be.

While they were out shopping that after-
noon, Hairy Bill would be in their house . . .
doing what? What did he do if the house
didn't need tidying? Did he read magazines?
Play computer games? Watch television?

And when the family were watching television that evening, Hairy Bill would be in the
house with them. Watching them.

And when Alex was sent to bed that night,
and went upstairs alone, and lay in bed alone

– Hairy Bill would be in the house then, too. He could stand over Alex's bed, watching him, and Alex wouldn't know whether he was there or not.

The thought gave Alex an unsettled, nervous feeling. He began to think that perhaps it wasn't such a great thing to have a ghost in the house.

Chapter 3
Things That Dust in the Night

For the second time in as many days, Alex was startled awake by his mother yelling. "Aaah! Rob! Aaah!"

She was on the landing outside his bedroom door. As he sat up in bed he heard his father, all bleary and sleepy. "Whassup?"

Alex slid out of bed and ran on to the landing. There was his mother, a pink dressing gown loosely belted round her, in bare feet and with her hair standing up in a tangle. She looked shocked and scared. Rob came out of their bedroom, wearing nothing but red boxer shorts and black socks. His wife turned into his arms. "I saw it!" she said. "I was coming across the landing when it came up the stairs with a duster in its hand."

Rob looked at Alex and started to laugh.

Kirsty punched him. "It's not funny!"

"I've heard of ghosts carrying their heads under their arms," Rob said, "but never a duster!"

"Don't laugh! I thought someone had broken in, and I was so scared I thought I was going to collapse—"

"Ah," Rob said, hugging her.

"And then I realized it was Hairy Bill. It's not pretty, I can tell you."

"What's it like?" Alex asked.

"You saw it," his mother said.

"Not its face. It was dark. All I could see was that it was hairy."

Kirsty nodded. "Short and hairy and – well,

I don't know. I couldn't really see its face for all the hair. It was just such a shock seeing something when I didn't expect it – and then it just vanished."

"Putting the clothes out didn't work, then," Rob said.

The night before, Kirsty had found a pair of Alex's old jeans, an old T-shirt and sweater and an old pair of shoes. She'd folded them all neatly and left them on the settee with a note. Alex had refused to help her write the note. He still wasn't sure that he wanted Hairy Bill to go.

"Anyway," he'd said, "what if it can't read?"

"I bet they have schools for bogles in Scotland," Rob had replied, jokingly. "I'm always being told Scotland has a better education system than England." He'd smiled at Kirsty.

"*Dear Hairy Bill*," she'd written on a sheet of notepaper. "*Thank you for tidying up.*

Here are some clothes for you. Hope you like them. Love, Kirsty, Rob and Alex."

But that had been the night before.

"Let's go downstairs," Alex said, "and see."

Rob went first, Kirsty second, and Alex last. The stairs and landing were unusually clean and tidy, but normal. Sunlight shone through the kitchen windows and reflected off clean and polished surfaces – wide, empty surfaces, because every dish and pot had been washed, every bottle and packet put away.

"Hairy's getting at me," Kirsty said, her hands on her hips. "It's saying I'm a bad housekeeper."

Rob opened the door of the living room, stuck his head in and said, "Oh, my—"

"What??"

"Calm down," Rob said. "Prepare for a shock."

"Oh, what?" Kirsty cried.

Alex squirmed past both of them, pressing himself against the door's lintel. He gaped.

Last night the walls of the room had been painted a pale, warm apricot. Now they were papered in dark red, with a crowded fleur-de-lis pattern in gold. The short, pale-blue curtains had been replaced by long ones, in dark red velvet with gold tassels. Covering the sofa was a large, tartan blanket. In one corner stood a tall, standard lamp that he'd never seen before.

He looked at the corner by the bay window. For a moment he thought the computer was gone, and his heart skipped. But the computer was still there, hidden beneath another tartan cloth.

"How in—?" Rob exclaimed.

"Bogles work hard," Kirsty said. "They used to harvest whole fields by themselves in one night."

Alex wandered across the room. The carpet felt softer and thicker, and he looked down. In place of their dark blue carpet was a black one. A square orange rug lay in front of the fire. "Where did this carpet come from?" he asked. "What's it done with our old one?"

"All this," Rob said, "and it found time to go round the house with a duster, too."

"If you want dusting done, Rob," Kirsty said, "you can use one just as well as me."

"Look," Alex said, and pointed.

Their little coffee table had gone. In its place, against one wall, was a large table, covered with a russet chenille cloth, with another lacy white cloth over it. On the table stood a large, green plant in a pot.

"That's an aspidistra," Rob said. "I think.

I didn't know anyone grew them any more."

Their gas fire was still in its place, but around it was a wooden mantelpiece, with a large, old-fashioned clock sitting in the middle of it, ticking loudly. A blue and white vase stood at either end. On the hearth below was a selection of brass fire-irons – poker, tongs, a little brush and shovel – even though none of them were needed for a gas fire.

Above the fireplace hung a big, dark picture. Alex went closer. Inside a large, golden, knobbly frame was a landscape: a grey, threatening sky above mountains, and a group of shaggy cattle with long horns. Alex knew, from holidays in Scotland, that they were Highland cattle.

Alex's father came to stand beside him. "Very Scottish baronial," he said. "Or, the best version of it that Hairy Bill could manage in a night."

"Look at this," Kirsty said. They turned and saw that she was by the settee, with its new tartan throw. Lying on top of the tartan were Alex's old clothes, still neatly folded. Kirsty held up the note she'd written.

Rob and Alex went over to see. Under Kirsty's message was another, in neat, but spiky handwriting. "*Dear Kirsty, your thanks are appreciated, but unnecessary. The clothes, though kindly meant, do not fit and are not required. I look forward to your longer acquaintance. Regards, Hairy.*"

Alex looked up at his mother in amazement. Rob laughed nervously. "I told you they had schools for bogles in Scotland!"

Kirsty said, "It's got to go."

"Oh, Mum!" Alex said.

Rob said, "Are you sure? I mean, decorating, washing-up, cleaning – all for a bowl of milk and a bit of bread—"

"I don't want . . . !" Kirsty yelled – she waved her arms at the room – "I don't want my rooms decorated in – in—!" She pointed at the painting of Highland cattle, and the tartan rug over the settee. "In Scottish baronial! I want my own stuff!" She flung out her arm to point at the standard lamp. "That belongs to Mrs Denby up the road. I've seen it in her house. She'll think we've stolen it!"

"Calm down," Rob said. "How is she going to know we haven't bought our own?"

"Then she'll think I'm copying her! And where has this stuff come from? No. It's got to go."

"Laying it with a present didn't work," Rob said. "So what now?"

Kirsty didn't answer. She strode over to the computer, snatched off the tartan cloth covering it, and switched it on.

"Looks like we're making the porridge again, Alex," Rob said.

"You are," Alex said. He went to stand behind his mother's chair, and watched her log on. She chose a search engine from 'favourites', and typed in 'house-blessing'.

"What's that mean?" he asked.

"Don't hang over my shoulder, it's annoying."

"But what are you looking for?" Alex said. "I might be able to help."

"I'm going to find someone who can crowbar Hairy out of here, and I don't need your help." The screen was filling with lists of sites already. She glanced over at Alex. "Have you done your homework?"

Alex groaned, but wandered off into the kitchen. He knew when he wasn't wanted.

Chapter 4

Miss Spellmaker

Alex said goodbye to his school friends at the corner. It was his last chance to shout out, "We've got a bogle!", but he didn't. He knew they wouldn't believe him, and would only jeer.

When he reached his gate, he stood outside for a long time, wondering if his mother was home yet. He didn't want to be alone with Hairy Bill. If it didn't show itself, then it would give him the creeps to know it was around somewhere – that it could be behind him, watching him. But he wasn't sure that he wanted to see it again either.

Don't be a coward, he told himself. None

of the stories said that bogles were dangerous ghosts – just mischievous at the worst. And he'd never find out if his mother was home by standing in the street.

He let himself in with his key. The hallway seemed narrower and darker than usual. Puzzled, he stood just inside the doorway, wondering if he'd somehow come to the wrong house.

The hall was darker because, while he'd been at school, it had been stripped and repainted in a dark choco-late brown. The carpet was different, too, and it was also brown. At the foot of the stairs, hanging on the wall, was a stuffed stag's head. Shutting the door, he said aloud, "Oh, this is too much!"

35

He dropped his school bag on the floor and shouted, hoping that Hairy Bill might hear, "We don't want dead deer's heads in our hall!"

Then he was scared that Hairy Bill would appear. His heart beat quicker. But nothing happened.

The bogle was about somewhere, though. Watching him from the landing, peering at him from the living room. Alex sent quick glances at both places, feeling nervier by the moment.

He took off his coat and hung it on the stair-post, before going into the kitchen to make himself a sandwich. Marmite toast was what he wanted, and he'd made the toast, buttered it, and was happily slapping on the marmite, when he sensed someone standing close behind him, and stiffened.

"I'll thank you," said a deep voice, "not to broadcast crumbs where I've just now cleaned."

Alex could see the bogle's brown hairiness, right next to him. He could look up from his toast and see its face, but he was afraid.

"And you've tracked in mud to spoil the nice rugs. Take off your shoes and leave them at the door," Hairy Bill said.

Alex looked up. The bogle's eyes glinted through hair that hung over a noseless face, and Alex felt a pang of horror. Then he told himself that its face was very like a hamster's, and not that frightening. It was just that you got a shock when you were expecting something more like a human face. "We never leave our shoes at the door."

"You'll leave them at the door now," said the bogle. "And you'll take your bag and coat upstairs, so you will." Before Alex could answer, the bogle turned away, and its broad, hairy brown back rapidly vanished from sight, as if it had hurried away down some long corridor that wasn't there. Its voice said, "I'll take them up for you the night, but after

that you've to do it yourself."

Alex ran down the
hall, Marmite toast
in hand. His coat
and his bag
were gone. In
fact, all the
coats were gone
from the hall.
Everyone would have to go upstairs to fetch
them whenever they wanted to go out. And
he'd have to go upstairs to fetch his bag when
he wanted to do his homework.

"You're dropping crumbs on my clean carpet!" said an angry voice in his ear, startling
him so much that he jumped. He was alone in
the hall. "Use a plate!" said the voice.

But he never used a plate and no one had
complained before. He began to see that his
mother and father had been right: having a
bogle in the house wasn't much fun.

A thought struck him and he went into the living room, still eating his toast. He wasn't halfway across the room before the toast was snatched from his hand and vanished. "Right!" Alex said.

The computer had not only been covered by a tartan blanket, it had been switched off and unplugged. Alex had to get down on his hands and knees to plug it in again. When it finally booted up, he went on-line and, from the list of favourite sites, he chose the one his mother had discovered, the Matheson family site.

The screen filled with tartan, and 'Scotland the Brave' played through the speakers. The site had news from Mathesons all over the world – chat about Highland Games in New South Wales and Manitoba, and bagpipe competitions in South Africa and Chile.

Afraid that Hairy Bill was breathing down his neck, Alex hastily typed a message into the bulletin board. *"Matheson family bogle needs good new home. Does housework.*"

Too much housework, he thought. Moving the cursor back, he typed "*originally from the Black Isle*" after "*bogle*". Then he went back to the end of what he'd written and typed, "*Any takers?*"

There was a loud knocking. Alex jumped, thinking it was Hairy Bill catching him out. He hurried to dispatch the message. The knocking came again. Someone was rapping sharply on the glass panels on the front door. Jumping up from his chair, Alex ran to answer it.

Outside, filling the doorway, was a suit of black motorcycling leathers. They were being worn by a short, fat person, who was pulling off a large, black crash helmet. When the helmet came off, he saw that it was a woman.

She had very black, very shiny hair, cut short. Her eyes were dark, and heavily made up with black eyeliner, drawn into a long point at the outer corners. It made the whites of her eyes seem very white, and they glared and stared. Her cheeks were healthily rosy, but she'd put on blueish lipstick. Through one dark eyebrow was a silver bar with a ball on each end. Another silver ball was stuck through the side of her nose, and another through her lower lip. In one ear was a golden sun, and in the other a silver moon. Alex had never seen anyone quite like her.

The woman smiled – a big, cheerful smile. "Blessings be, Sunshine."

"What?"

The woman laughed. "Blessings be. It's what us witches say. Is there a Kirsty Matheson round here?"

"She's my mum."

"Praise the Goddess! Is she in, your mum?"

"Er – no. But she should be back soon."

"Cool! Would you like to see my motor-bike?"

"Er – why not?" Alex said, still feeling stunned.

"Excellent!" she said, with another big smile, holding out a black-gloved hand to shake. "I'm Olly Spellmaker. What do I call you?"

They shook hands. "Alex. Alex Langford – that's my dad's name. I call myself Matheson sometimes, if I feel like it."

"Good thinking, to have two names," said Olly, as they went down the path. "You can call yourself whatever you like, y'know, so long as you're not trying to cheat people. Here's the bike."

She hardly needed to point it out. It was standing at the kerb, nearly as big as a small car, gleaming black and silver. The fuel tank was painted with a stormy sky, split with lightning, and the word, 'Stormrider'. The painting and lettering was mostly black and silver too, except for some blue and green.

"A big improvement on broomsticks, eh?" Olly said.

Alex nodded, but privately thought it was a bit silly of her to paint her bike up like that. She was a fat little woman riding a motorbike, not a witch riding a storm.

"So," Olly said, "how are you getting on with the boggart?"

"The what?"

"Brownie? Bogle? Different folks call 'em different things." Alex was staring at her in surprise. "Your mother emailed me about it."

Alex looked nervously over his shoulder towards the house.

"It's cool," Olly said. "That's why I brought us out here. They keep pretty much to the house, y'know, once they're in. I doubt if it's listening to us now."

"It's bossy," Alex said. "It keeps making all sorts of new rules. It's like having two mothers!"

Olly grimaced. "Let me see your hand."

Puzzled, and a little wary, Alex held out his hand. She turned his hand over and looked at his palm. "Oh, cool! You could be a witch, y'know."

"Give over!" Alex snatched his hand back.

"No word of a lie. I thought there might be

somebody like you in the case. Bogles are like poltergeists, y'see."

"No," Alex said.

"Poltergeists – noisy ghosts – chuck things about, bang on walls, make a nuisance of themselves. Where you find

a poltergeist, you nearly always find a young-  ster with the makings of a witch. And here you are."

Alex felt embarrassed. He was very ordinary and unmagical. He'd never done anything remotely magical in his entire life.

"Ah," Olly said, "here's your mother."

Alex looked up and saw his mother's rusty little Fiat coming down the road. "How did you know that was my mother?"

Olly glanced at him and grinned. "I've been a witch a lot longer than you have."

The Fiat struggled to manoeuvre into a small parking space a little further up the road, and they strolled over to meet it. As Kirsty clambered out of the car, Alex said, "Mum, there's a lady here—"

"Olly Spellmaker," said Olly, leaning past Alex and holding out her hand. "Blessings be. You asked me to take a dekka at the old homestead."

Kirsty stared at Olly's piercings, the leathers, the earrings. "Oh. Yes. Hello, Miss Spellmaker."

"Olly. Can I help you carry anything in?"

"Oh, no, no." Kirsty locked up the car, and they went back to the house. "I suppose you've heard of bogles?"

"And you're Scottish!" Olly said, clapping her gloved hands together. "Yep! It all makes sense!"

"Well, you see—" Kirsty pushed open the front door, which Alex had left open a crack. "My great-aunt died and—" She broke off as she stepped into the hall. Swinging round, she said, "Alex, did you do this?"

"Oh, Mum, give me a break. I re-decorated the hall since I got back from school? And if I had, I wouldn't have done it like this."

She dropped her bag beside his, and put her hand to her head. "Alex, I'm sorry. I'm going round the twist."

Olly Spellmaker had gone past them into the kitchen. "Oh, yes!" She unzipped her jacket. "I can feel it – the presence. It's a real humdinger." She went into the living room in her big boots, taking off her jacket to reveal a scarlet blouse.

"Can you get rid of it?" Kirsty asked, following her.

Olly looking surprised. "You want to get rid of it?"

Kirsty spread her arms. "Look at what it's done to my house!"

Olly looked round. "I like it. Cosy."

"I don't want cosy!" Kirsty said. "If I'd

wanted cosy, I'd never have left the Black Isle!"

Without being asked, Olly threw herself down in one of the big leather armchairs by the hearth. "But, Mrs Matheson – can I call you Kirsty? What you've got here is a benevolent house spirit. Guardian of the house and home. A luck bringer. A real strong one too. A real old, strong one. You'd be mad to get rid of it."

"But it wants me to take my shoes off and leave them at the door!" Alex said. "And use a plate for my toast – and take my bag and coat upstairs every day – and it unplugged the computer!"

"You've changed your tune," his mother said.

"I'm fed up of it," Alex said.

"Oh, come on!" Olly Spellmaker leaned back in the chair and clasped her hands behind her head. "It might take a while to shakedown with each other, but it'll be worth it!"

"Let me ask *you*, Miss Spellmaker," said Kirsty. "Have you ever lived with a bogle?"

"Just give me the chance! I'd love—"

"You haven't," Kirsty said. "My family has. Luck-bringers and guardians of the home they may be, but they're also pains in the neck! Unmitigated nuisances! Look at all this stuff! Look at those armchairs!"

Olly, with surprise, looked at the armchair she was sitting in.

"They're not mine!" Kirsty shouted. "Where did they come from? What do I say if the real owner turns up?" She calmed down and stopped shouting. "I don't want to argue about this. I just want to be rid of the thing. If you can't get rid of it, or don't want to, just say so, and I'll find someone else."

Olly stood, raising her hands. "Don't get upset, Mrs Matheson, please. If you want me to cast the spirit out, I'll cast it out. I just think it's a shame, because everyone is getting rid of their bogles these days—"

"Are they?" Alex said. Three days ago, he hadn't even known that people had them, let alone that they were getting rid of them.

"Oh, casting 'em out in all directions. If you're in the know, you hear about it."

"How long will it take?" Kirsty asked.

"Hard to say." Olly stood in the middle of the hearth rug, under the painting of Highland cattle, and stretched her arms above her head. "I'll just limber up. And then I'll have to concentrate, to tune in—"

A deep, strange voice cut in. "We'll not be having any of that!"

They all jumped. Olly spun round because the voice came from behind her.

Sitting in the leather armchair by the fire was something like a very large Yorkshire terrier, if Yorkshire terriers were reddish-brown. Hidden under the hair was a short, broad man-like thing, sitting cross-legged. Its face was hard to see because tangled hair hung in front of it, but quick, bright eyes kept gleaming as it looked from one to another of them. Alex quickly moved closer to his mother.

Olly pointed at Hairy Bill and said, "Spirit, I command you—"

"Away with yer, and button your lip!" said Hairy Bill. "I need no help to speak with Mathesons." It lifted one short, powerful, hairy arm and pointed to Kirsty. "You, lassie. Come and sit you down here." It pointed to the other armchair.

Kirsty took Alex's arm and went to the empty armchair. She almost fell into it, and then hugged Alex to her.

"Don't worry," Olly said. "I won't let it hurt you."

"Och!" said Hairy. "Won't you, now?" The bogle looked across at Kirsty and Alex. "Old I am, old. I've seen seas dry and forests wither. Time out of mind I've worked for the Mathesons as a shepherd works for sheep. And so you tell me now that you want me to leave you?"

"Yes!" Kirsty cried.

"You break our bond?" said the bogle.

"Yes!"

"So be it!" said the bogle and clapped its brown, hairy hands together with a noise so loud it was startling. They jumped, blinked – and the armchair was empty.

Alex jumped up. "That was easy!"

Kirsty looked at Olly in some embarrassment. "I seem to have wasted your time, Miss

Spellmaker, and I'm sorry about that." She frowned at the armchairs and the painting over the mantelpiece. "It might have taken all its junk with it!"

"Oh, it hasn't gone," Olly said. Both Alex and his mother stared at her. "It might want you to think it's gone, but it hasn't. It's hiding."

"How do you know?" Kirsty asked.

"Do you think I'm spinning you a tale?" Olly replied. "Trying to get paid for banishing old Hairy when he's already gone?"

"Something like that," Kirsty said, and Alex said, "Mum!"

"I'm sensitive," Olly said. Standing there in her big boots and motorbike leathers, she didn't look sensitive. "I feel things. That's why I'm a witch. And I can feel that he's still here."

"Then I think what we should do," Kirsty said, "is to say goodbye now, and if we have any more trouble, I'll contact you again."

"Cool," Olly said. "If that's what you want to do."

"Can I give you some money towards your petrol?" Kirsty asked.

Olly shook her head as she put on her jacket. The piercings in her nose and lip caught the light, and it seemed to Alex that there was something different about it. He looked round the room, but couldn't see what was making the difference.

"I think I'll be seeing you again, soon," Olly said, as she picked up her helmet. "We can talk about what you owe me then."

"I'll see you out," Kirsty said. "Thank you so much for coming."

Olly went into the hall first, with Kirsty following, and Alex tagging after her, feeling rather sorry that Olly was going, and wishing that he could ask her more about being a witch.

Olly opened the front door, came to a full halt, and swore. Kirsty looked over her shoulder and made a noise that was something between a gasp and a small scream.

"What?" Alex said. "What is it?" He couldn't see past them, and they wouldn't move.

He ran back into the living room and went to the window. Lifting up the net curtains he looked out and saw—

Chapter 5
The Bargain

Outside the window was a beautiful Scottish glen, with mountains, a blue sky high above, and a brown stream among rocks.

The pavements, the lamp-posts, the privet hedges, the brick houses, the parked cars – they'd all gone.

Alex backed away from the window in alarm, at the same time that Olly and his mother came bundling back into the room. "Where's everything gone? Where are we? How is Dad going to find us?"

"Don't freak out!" Olly said. "It's cool. I think this is just a glamour."

"A what?" Alex said. He thought 'glamour' meant photographs in magazines of models wearing expensive clothes.

"I mean, it's just a spell cast to make things look different." She peered through the window. "It's not really wild country out there. It's still the street – and my bike. Hairy's just made it look different."

Alex joined her and looked outside again. He watched a couple of sheep, their dirty, unravelling fleeces dragging behind them, make their way down to the stream. "Looks pretty real to me," he said.

"Oh, Hairy's *good*," Olly said.

"I'm going upstairs," Kirsty said, and clumped noisily up them.

Alex had a thought and went through to the back of the house, to the kitchen. Olly followed him. "Now what's out there," Alex said, pointing to the door as they went into the kitchen, "is a yard and a shed, and a bit of a lawn and some flowers." He opened the door.

A sheep stood a couple of feet away, looking at them solemnly while it chewed. It stood in a tangle of long grass and bilberries. Behind it was a vast expanse of moorland, and dark mountains, and a grey sky above. There was no sign of the shed, or the neighbours' houses, or any wooden fences or hedges.

"He's *very* good," Olly said. "But then, he's a bogle."

Kirsty came clattering downstairs again. "It's the same on all sides, for as far as you can see. Just mountains and wilderness. I can't even see a road. You say this is just a glamour?"

Olly raised her brows, her silver piercing glinting. "I said your Hairy was a strong one. Really strong. He must be well old."

Kirsty put her hands on her hips. "Any ideas?" Her voice, Alex noticed, was sharp and edgy.

Olly wandered back into the living room. Hands in pockets, she stood looking through the window at the mountains and the sheep. "Go fishing?"

"You're supposed to be the expert in these things!" Kirsty shouted. "Do something! Get us back home! Alex has school in the morning! I've got to go to work!"

Olly raised her hands in a peace-making way. "Mrs Matheson, this is as new to me as it is to you. I've cleared houses of spirits, I've talked to unhappy ghosts and sent them on their way, I've had a lot of odd experiences, but I've never come across anything quite like Hairy Bill before."

Kirsty looked as if she was going to throw things. Alex said quickly, "Can't we get Hairy to come back – somehow? And talk to him?"

"I was going to suggest that," Olly said. "We can try. I think if we all stand in a circle and hold hands . . . Come on, come on." She waved to them.

Alex and Kirsty shuffled into place alongside her, darting glances at each other and feeling embarrassed. Olly snatched a hand

from each of them. "Hold hands!" she said. They held hands, feeling like idiots.

"Oh, house spirit," Olly said, in a deeper voice than usual. Alex looked at her in surprise, then looked at his mother. Both of them nearly laughed. "Oh, spirit that dwells in this house, hear me . . ."

"I can hear yer!" said Hairy Bill's voice. They whipped round. He was sitting, again, in his armchair. He waved a hairy hand at Olly. "It's with the Mathesons I have business. It was and is always with the Mathesons I have business."

Olly looked at the other two, and then stepped aside. "I'm still here," she whispered.

Alex nodded. Where else would she go?

"You Mathesons," said Hairy Bill. "You ken where you are?"

Kirsty said, "The Black Isle?"

"Aye," said the bogle. "The Black Isle, that you never should have left."

"I had to leave," Kirsty said. "There was nothing—"

"You never should have left!" boomed the bogle, and Kirsty was quiet. "The Mathesons have been in the Black Isle since before it was the Black Isle, since before they were Mathesons. Since there were people on this land at all, they've been there. And the first people, they called on me, and they made a bargain. I gave them help – I gathered luck for them, and guarded them – and they gave me blood. And flesh."

Kirsty reached out and took Alex's hand. Her grip was tight and her skin sweaty. He saw her send a quick, anxious look at Olly.

"They gave me a boy," said Hairy Bill, and he looked at Alex. "They buried him in my earth. For long, long years after that – and I have seen forests grow and wither – they gave me blood every year, in memory of that first bargain. They cut the throat of a calf or sheep and let its blood pour on my ground – or, if no animal was to be spared, they cut their own arms and let their own blood fall."

Neither Kirsty nor Alex dared to speak. Not even Olly made a sound.

"But times change and grow soft," said the bogle. "They gave me no more blood, but beer or wine instead. Not so good, but I was kind. Still I guarded them and brought them luck. And then it was no longer even beer, but only bread and milk – and they thought they were hard served, these folk, giving up a little piece of bread and a bowl of milk! But still I was kind, still I worked for them, still I watched over them, because I had made a bargain. Even when they left me and went away, still I worked for them, still I followed them – followed them from my land into

64

places that were hateful. Still I was faithful.

"But now you want to break the bargain. You wish to forget all my service, all my labour. Very well, madam. Let it be so. But there is a price to pay. You must pay me again the price that sealed the bargain." The bogle's eyes gleamed through its hair as it looked at Alex. "You must give me blood, and flesh. You must give me that boy, there, to bury in my earth."

Chapter 6
The Dragon and the Mouse

Kirsty's hand tightened so much on Alex's fingers that it hurt. "No," she said.

"You refuse me again?" said the bogle.

"You win," Kirsty said. "If that's what it takes to get rid of you – then make yourself at home!" She laughed, high-pitched and unsteady.

"I'm tired of serving ungrateful mortals," the bogle said. "Go back to your city. I shall stay here – and take my pay." The bogle sprang from the chair, straight at Alex.

Alex saw the bogle coming at him through the air – slowly, it seemed, and yet there wasn't time to duck or run away. The bogle's hair flew upward to show glittering dark eyes, fierce, like a cat's. Its mouth opened to show teeth. Its hooked fingers had long nails, or claws.

Something shoved in front of him, knocking him over backwards. He hit the floor with a thump and a grunt as the breath was knocked out of him.

His mother came down on top of him, shouting his name. For a moment they rolled on the floor together, shouting and gasping for breath, and it was hard to know what was going on. Then Alex sorted himself out – he was on the floor beside one of the leather armchairs, his mother was on top of him, and they could both see the bogle hopping up and down in its chair, dodging from side to side.

It was dodging a dragon. There was a dragon in the house. Its colour kept shimmering between red and green, and it was quite fat, and as it flapped its wings and bounced from side to side, trying to stop the bogle from reaching them, it puffed and snorted a

lot, as if out of breath. The dragon, Alex realized, was Olly.

Olly wasn't anywhere in the room – that was one reason for thinking it. And then, the dragon *looked* like Olly. Not only was it fat, but its greeny-reddish skin was shiny and leathery, like Olly's motorcycle leathers.

The bogle made shooing motions, and went, "Tch!", but the dragon bobbed and bounced and jumped in its way so determinedly that Hairy Bill couldn't get past.

"Come on," Kirsty said to Alex, on her hands and knees, about to crawl away.

"Where?" Alex said. He couldn't think of anywhere they could hide from the bogle. Outside was a wilderness of sheep. Besides, it would be cowardly to leave Olly by herself.

The dragon drew a long breath, which rattled and choked in a phlegmy way. "Huuuur!" the dragon said, and breathed out fire.

It was a long, thin thread of fire that missed

the bogle and hit the painting of highland cattle over the mantelpiece. Hairy Bill stopped
trying to reach Alex, and stared. "My painting!" he cried. Then he pounced again, but
this time at the dragon, making a long, swinging swipe with hooked fingers.

Brighter red stripes appeared on the
dragon's side, and giving a frightened yelp
that sounded like, "Ack!", it blundered away
towards the other end of the room. Hairy Bill
grabbed its tail and hauled, swinging it
round.

"Alex!" the dragon cried – an appeal for
help.

Alex started forward, but then stopped. He
knew that he couldn't be of any help, that the
bogle was much stronger, in every way, than
he was.

I wish, I wish, he thought, and he wished so
hard that the very force of wishing seemed to
sway him on his feet. I *wish* I was . . . was . . .
a lion! A tiger! A bear!

He wished so hard that he scowled, his teeth clenched, his fists balled tight, even his toes curled. He wished so hard that it hurt – a strange, twisty pain at the centre of him that seemed to fold him closer to the floor. Then he was scuttling across it, determined to sink teeth and claws into Hairy Bill and make him let Olly the dragon go.

He ran against Hairy Bill's hairy leg and scraped at it with his hand – which had become an odd, neat little fingered paw – but the scratching didn't have much effect. Hairy Bill was protected by so much hair. Alex tried his teeth, and Hairy Bill looked down, laughed, and said, "Ah, Mousey!"

Mousey? Wasn't he a lion, then?

"Alex! Look out!"

That was Olly. Hairy Bill had let Olly go all right. Hairy Bill was now leaning over the arm of one of the leather armchairs, and had taken the shape of a big, a very big, tiger-striped tabby cat with glaring green eyes, its ears laid flat with threat and spite.

"Alex – run!"

Alex was already running. He ran around the armchair, trying to get underneath, to hide. But he couldn't get underneath. His back hit the chair. He was too big. He couldn't understand it – a mouse that was too big to get under a chair? Or was he changing shape again?

Turning quickly, he ran across the floor towards the door, hoping to escape into the hall. He felt his back humping as he scuttled, and his tail upraised behind him, and then

something big landed with a soft thump in front of him – something big and striped, with a mad green glare and teeth. Alex's claws trod hard into the carpet as he tried to stop and turn. He squeaked and whisked round, his tail whipping behind him. Maybe he could hide behind the chair.

Kirsty's voice shouted, "It's on top of the chair!"

Alex took a quick glimpse upwards. There was the big, fierce cat, perched on the high back of the leather armchair, eagerly watching for Alex to come close enough for him to drop down on his back, claws out . . .

There was a reddish lumbering in the air – a feather dropped, and a hen was flapping and dipping as it struggled through the air between Alex and the cat.

The cat sprang from the back of the chair into the middle of the room. It leaped and, in mid-air, changed into Hairy Bill again. And Hairy Bill, reaching out a hand, snatched the hen from the air. The hen hung by its neck from Hairy Bill's fist, pathetically kicking its legs and flapping its wings.

Alex, in a panic, felt his mouse shape fall from him – he felt himself unfolding and rising up, in his own shape again. "Don't hurt her!"

"I shall have her blood," Hairy Bill said. "I shall have yours. I shall dye my clothes red

with it. And when travellers come here, to
this house, I shall freshen the red of my
clothes with their blood."

Hairy Bill raised the hen to his
mouth, baring his teeth.

Alex started forward,
meaning to try and grab
the hen from him,
and, from the

other end of the room, Kirsty reached out,
crying, "Alex!"

And the computer went, 'Beep!'

"What?" Hairy Bill lowered the struggling, croaking hen. "What was that?"

"The computer!" Alex said, pulling his mother towards it. "Someone knows where we are! Someone'll help us!"

Seizing the computer mouse, he logged on. The computer sang its little tune as it dialled the server, and then the card came up asking for a password.

Alex could feel that Hairy Bill had drawn closer, perhaps curious. The bogle still held the flapping hen that was Olly. Wasn't she able to change back into her own shape?

Alex typed in his password, his nervous fingers mistyping so that he had to delete letters and try again. His skin prickled with anxiety. Every second he expected to feel Hairy Bill's clawed fingers on him, or to hear poor Olly hen squawk as her neck was wrung.

The computer accepted the password. It seemed to take an age for the email screen to load. "*You have one unread email in your inbox.*" Alex clicked, and the screen jumped to the in-box.

Holding his breath, he clicked on the unread email, and read it aloud.

"*Hi, fellow Matheson! Rory Matheson here, hailing from Nova Scotia, Canada. You got a bogle? A real, Matheson, house-cleaning Black Isle bogle from the old country? I want him! Can give him a good home. See photos in attachment. We got space, we got fir trees, horses, cattle. Got kids, too, and too much work for one family to manage. I got dibs on that bogle!*"

"Mathesons?" said Hairy Bill, and let go of the hen.

There was a thump, and Alex looked down to see Olly and her motorcyle leathers emerging from a tangle of red feathers. Olly lay slumped on the floor, not moving. "Are you all right?" Alex called.

Hairy Bill was hemming him in at the

computer. The bogle was as hairy as a tangled old sheepskin, and smelt like an old rug, too – of burning, dogs and tobacco. "Show me the photographs," it said.

Alex clicked on the paperclip symbol, to open the attachment file. "It'll take ages to load," he said. "Wait. Keep watching." And while Hairy Bill watched the computer screen, Alex ducked down and crawled across the floor to see how Olly was.

Kirsty was already with her, and Olly was propping herself up on one elbow. "I'm OK, I'm OK," she said, though she looked white and not well at all. Her voice was hoarse – probably as a result of having been clutched round the neck while she was shaped like a hen, Alex thought. "It just takes it out of you – changing like that. And I gave it all I'd got."

"You were great," Alex said. "Especially the dragon. How do you change into a dragon?"

Olly pulled a face and clutched at her belly.

"Don't try it. It hurts. I feel like I've been run over by a truck. And we're not out of the wood yet."

She looked at the bogle. Alex and Kirsty looked too. Hairy Bill was still standing in front of the computer screen, staring. They looked at each other, and then quietly crawled away to the other end of the room, where they hid behind one of the big armchairs and peered out.

"Wonderful!" Hairy Bill said suddenly. He wasn't speaking to them, but to the computer screen, or to himself. "Mathesons! It could be the old Black Isle."

He whirled round and reached high into the air as if stretching. From the air he grabbed a large rucksack with one hand and a set of bagpipes with the other. Spinning round again, he vanished in mid-twirl.

Chapter 7
Blessings Be

The floor beneath Alex heaved as if it had hiccups. He saw the big painting of Highland cattle falling, and ducked, hiding his head – but the expected crash of breaking frame and glass never came. Instead there was another sound: a sort of whoosh! And a fizzling, sizzling noise, as if everything was dissolving like a glass of soluble aspirin.

Alex folded his arms over his head and huddled up small until the noise stopped. Even then, he didn't dare to move. He wondered about opening one eye and peeping out from the shelter of his arms, but was scared of what he might see. His house and everything might have disappeared. There

might be nothing but nothingness.

Then he heard Ollie say, "It's OK, it's cool. I think it's over."

Cautiously Alex unwound his arms and lifted his head. He saw his mother looking round, her face already flinching, her eyes ready to squeeze shut.

The red wallpaper hung from the walls in strips. The dark blue carpet was ruckled up in waves, as if it had tried to lift itself up and leave, but had been weighed down by the furniture. The painting from over the mantelpiece was gone, nowhere to be seen. One of the big leather armchairs had been thrown over, the other was split, with stuffing bulging from it.

Alex got to his feet. His mother reached for him. "Oh, Alex, no . . ."

Olly clambered to her feet too. "It's cool, Mrs Matheson. Hairy Bill really has gone. I can feel it."

Alex realized that he could feel it too. He

hadn't really thought about it before, or put it into words, but all the time Hairy Bill had been with them, there had been a sort of faint buzzing in his ears, a sensation of the room being fuller than it was, of the air being thicker. However you tried to describe the feeling, now it was gone. "It's quieter than it was," he said.

"That's it," Olly said, and gave him a look like a teacher who's pleased that a pupil has been quick to understand something. "That's why we call a haunted house 'an unquiet house'."

Alex crossed the room to the window. He nearly tripped over their old coffee table, which had reappeared. The big table had gone, though the tablecloths that had covered it were crumpled on the floor. The window was curtainless.

Outside, he could see the pavement. In their front yard, staring at him with amazed yellow eyes, was a black-faced sheep. Nearby was the large aspidistra plant that had stood on the big table, toppled over in its pot. Beyond, in the road, was the tall, standard lamp.

Kirsty had got to her feet and was looking round at the mess. "How are we ever going to get this straight?"

"What shall we do with the sheep?" Alex asked. A second sheep had joined the first, trotting round from the back of the house. His mother joined him at the window and peered out at the animals in dismay. "Can we keep them?" Alex asked.

"No!" She turned to Olly. "Can't you send them back?"

"In a van," Olly said.

"But you turned into a dragon! And a mouse!" Alex and Olly looked at each other, then quickly away. Neither told Kirsty that she was mistaken about the mouse. "You can send a couple of little sheep back to Scotland, surely!"

"The shape-changing was glamour," Olly

said, "and I'm not very good at it. I could carry those sheep to Scotland easier than I could magic them there. Sorry."

"You're not much use, are you?" Kirsty said, and Alex said, "Mum!"

Olly sighed. "Look. Let's have a sit-down, a cup of coffee and a sandwich, and I'll see what I can do."

Alex went into the hall and opened the front door. He wanted to make sure the street was real and solid.

The sheep took fright and scuttered about the yard, their fleeces bouncing, looking for a way to escape him. He circled round them, making them think he was trying to come up behind them, so they ran together down the passage to the back of the house, their hoofs clattering on the paving slabs.

Alex went out on to the street, carefully closing the gate behind him. He didn't want the sheep to get into the road.

He walked towards the standard lamp. Coming down the street towards him was their neighbour, Mrs Denby. She was small and thin, with bluish white hair in tight curls, and she wore a flowered dress with a little cardie over it. They met, in the middle of the road, by the standard lamp, which stood there with its plug trailing on the tarmac. Together they looked at it for a while.

"I think that's my lamp," Mrs Denby said.

"Do you?" Alex asked.

"It used to stand in my corner, behind my chair."

"What's it doing out here?" Alex asked.

"I'm sure I don't know, if you don't. It went missing days ago. Just went. I thought I'd been broke into. I got on to the police, and they sent a constable round, but he couldn't find anywhere that anybody had got in. 'So where's my lamp gone, then?' I said. He said he didn't know. And now here it is. It is mine, you know. I'm sure it is."

"Shall I carry it into your house for you?" Alex asked.

"Well, if you'd be so good, I should be grateful."

When Alex came back, Olly was leaning on the gate. "We've phoned the RSPCA about the sheep," she said.

"What about the mess in there?" Alex asked, nodding towards the house.

"Your mother's already planning the new décor."

Alex groaned, foreseeing a painful disruption ahead while carpets were laid and walls scraped and new paper put up.

"What about you?" Olly asked.

Alex looked puzzled.

"Have you ever changed shape before?" she asked.

For a few moments, Alex looked back with amazement at what he had done. "Never. But I never wanted to so much before."

"Having me and Hairy around probably helped," Olly said. "Magic in the air, and all that. Still, what you did, that was really cool for a beginner."

"I'm glad it's over," Alex said. "I don't

think I want to do anything like that again."

"What a waste! I could teach you a lot."

"I wanted to turn into a lion – and I turned into a mouse. What if I turned into some nasty bug by mistake? What if I got stuck?"

"That's why I think you should learn more about it," Olly said.

"I wasn't planning on being a witch. I was thinking of being a webmaster or a games scripter."

"Let me give you this, then." From her leathers, Olly took a little card and handed it to him. There was a website address printed on it. "That's our on-line coven."

"Coven?"

"A witches' get-together." Olly came out from behind the gate, putting her helmet on. "Keep in touch. Blessings be, sunshine. Be seeing you."

When he couldn't hear the din of her motorbike any more, Alex went round to the back garden, where he sat on the doorstep and watched the black-faced sheep crop their bit of lawn, until he heard his father shout hello to a neighbour.

When he turned the corner of the house, his father was just turning his key in the lock. "Hiya, son! Had a good day?"

"OK," Alex said. "Hairy's gone, by the way."

"Oh, good!" Rob went through the front door into the wreckage of the hall, and caught a glimpse, through the kitchen window, of the back garden. "Alex! Do you know anything about those sheep?"